For
Mum and Dad, brother Ben,
and Alice
J. F.

First U.S. edition 2008

Library of Congress Cataloging-in-Publication Data is available.

Library of Congress Catalog Card Number pending

ISBN 978-0-7636-3657-9

2 4 6 8 10 9 7 5 3 1

Printed in China

This book was typeset in Gill Sans.
The illustrations were done in charcoal, colored pencil, and pastel.

Candlewick Press
2067 Massachusetts Avenue
Cambridge, Massachusetts 02140

visit us at www.candlewick.com

Say Hello

Jack & Michael Foreman

CANDLEWICK PRESS
CAMBRIDGE, MASSACHUSETTS

Left out.

All alone.

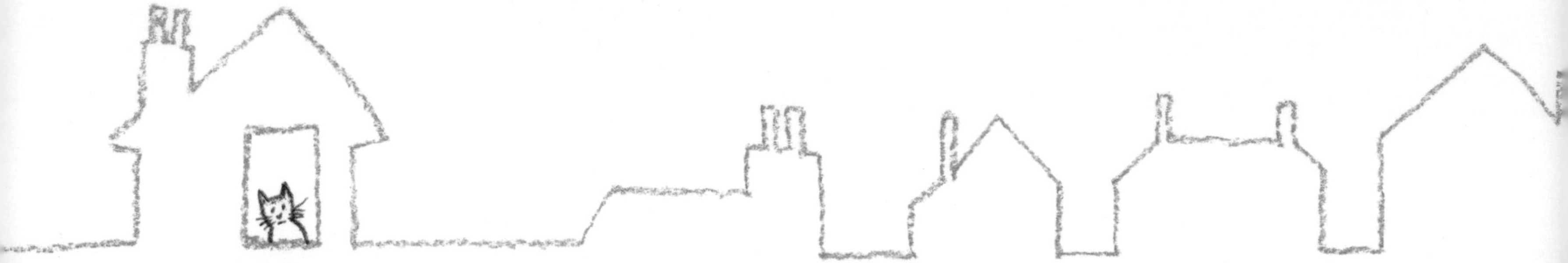

No friend, no home.

What's this?

Can I play too?

It's great to make new friends like you!

Left out, no fun.

Why am I the only one?

Left out, no fun.

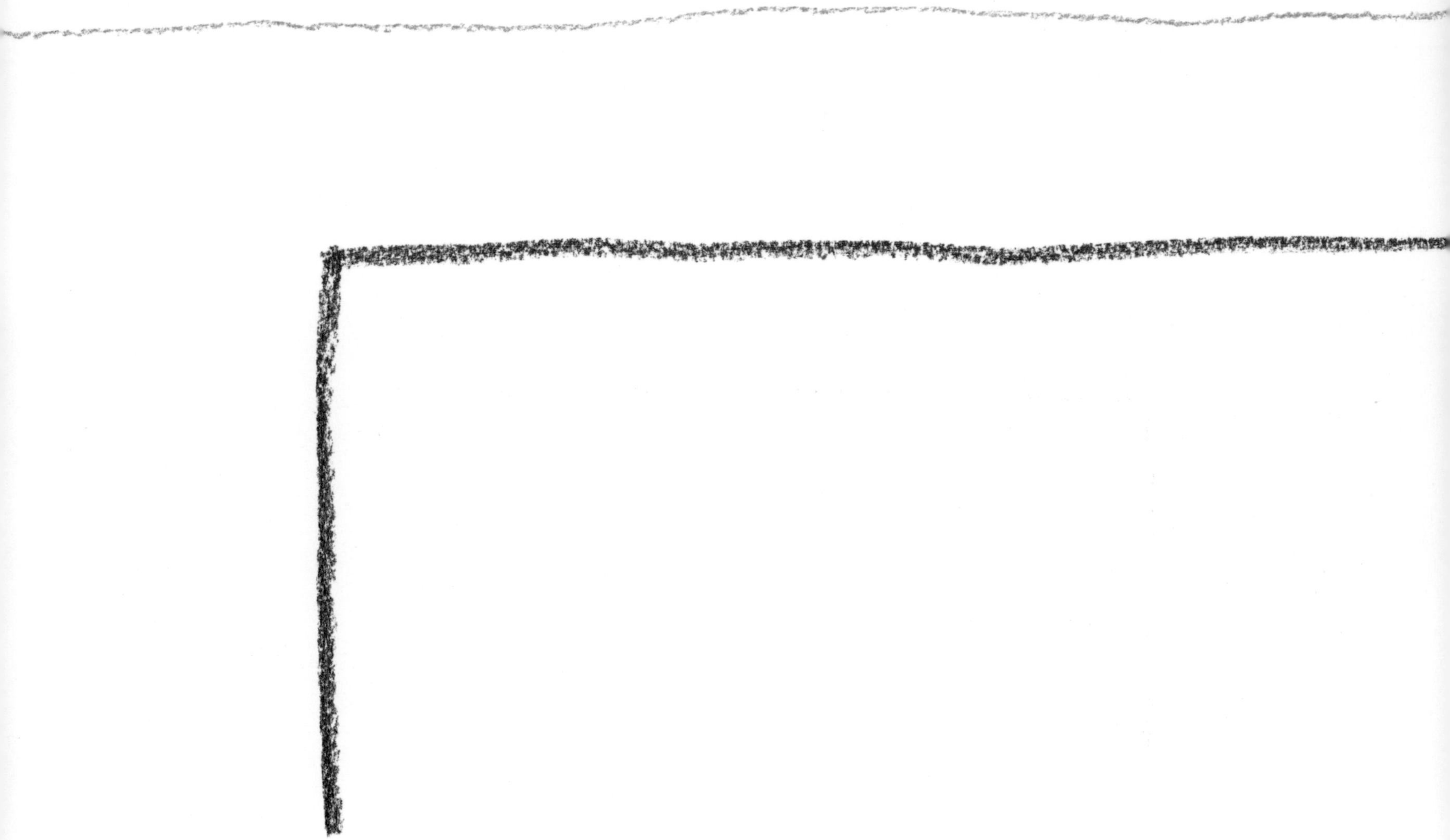

Why am I the lonely one?

Left out, no fun.

I wouldn't do this

to anyone.

What’s this?

Come and join the fun!

No need to be the lonely one.

When someone's feeling left out, low,

it doesn't take much to say . . .

Hello!

Aloha! Shalom!

Namaste!

Szia! Dia duit! Ciao!

Ave!

Konichiwa! Olá! Kia ora!

Sveiki!

Hellow! Labas! Hej! Sekoh! Cześć!

Hola! Привет! 你好

Jambo! Salaam! Helō!